To my Aunt Roz for teaching my daughter
how to love dogs. —L.R.

To all artists who fill this world with
their wonderful imaginations. —C.E.

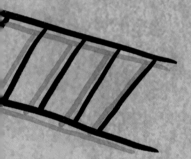

KAR-BEN PUBLISHING
A division of Lerner Publishing Group, Inc.
241 First Avenue North
Minneapolis, MN 55401 USA
1-800-4-KARBEN

Website address: www.karben.com

Main body text set in Zemke Hand ITC Std 18/24.
Typeface provided by International Typeface Corp.

Library of Congress Cataloging-in-Publication Data

Rose, Lisa, author.
    Shmulik paints the town / by Lisa Rose ; illustrated by Catalina Echeverri.
       pages cm
    Summary: "Shmulik, a town artist, is commissioned to paint a mural for Yom Ha'atzma'ut but
can't   haf to paint. Luckily, he gets some help from an unlikely collaborator - his dog!"—Provided by
publisher.
    ISBN 978-1-4677-5239-8 (lb : alk. paper) — ISBN 978-1-4677-5249-7 (pb : alk. paper)
    ISBN 978-1-4677-9607-1 (eb pdf)
    [1. Independence Day (Israel)—Fiction. 2. Artists—Fiction. 3. Dogs—Fiction.]
I. Echeverri, Catalina, 1986- illustrator. II. Title.
PZ7.1.R6695Sh 2015
[E]—dc23
                                                2015017055

Manufactured in the United States of America
1 — CG — 10/1/15

Shmulik Paints the Town

Lisa Rose

Illustrated by
Catalina Echeverri

KAR-BEN
PUBLISHING

On Monday, the mayor visited Shmulik the painter.

"Soon it will be Yom Ha'Atzmaut, and we will celebrate Israel's independence. Can you paint us a mural on the wall and decorate the park around it?"

"Certainly!" said Shmulik.

"Everyone from the town will be there," the mayor went on. "There will be awards and speeches. There will be music and dancing. There will be flags and fireworks."

"Wonderful! I can't wait to get started," said Shmulik.

On Tuesday, Shmulik and his dog, Ezra,
walked to the mural wall.

"I can't think of anything to paint, Ezra. So today I'll just look up at the sky and be inspired by the puffy cloud shapes."

On Wednesday, Shmulik and Ezra walked to the mural wall.

"I can't think of anything to paint, Ezra," said Shmulik. "I'll just take a walk around the park and get inspired by the lovely trees."

"I'll paint tomorrow, Ezra."

On Thursday, Shmulik and Ezra walked to the mural wall.

"I still can't think of anything to paint, Ezra," said Shmulik. "But I know it will come to me. Meanwhile I'll feed this hungry kitten and get inspired by her soft purrs."

"I think the mural can wait till tomorrow, Ezra."

On Friday, Shmulik and Ezra walked to the mural wall.

"I still can't think of anything to paint, Ezra. I'm getting a little worried. And I'm hungry. I'll go to the bakery and buy my challah for Shabbat."

"I'll think about what to paint over Shabbat," said Shmulik when he came back from the bakery.

The next day was Shabbat. Shmulik rested. Even Ezra rested.

On Sunday, Shmulik cried, "What am I going to do, Ezra? Everyone wants to see the wall filled with beautiful art but I still don't know what I'm going to paint!"

"All this thinking is making me tired, Ezra. I'll take a short nap. Maybe my dreams will help."

Shmulik woke up and rubbed his eyes. "Wow! Am I dreaming? These are masterpieces. Did I paint these in my sleep? Was I finally inspired in my dreams? I must be very talented."

But then he noticed something . . .

"Oh my! I can't believe it! Was it you, Ezra?" asked Shmulik.

"Ruff!" barked Ezra.

Soon, people began gathering for the Yom Ha'Atzmaut celebration.

Everyone was amazed by the paintings all over the park.

"This is the most beautiful art our town has ever had!" exclaimed the mayor. "Todah rabah. Thank you so much, Shmulik!"

"But it wasn't me—it was my dog," said Shmulik.

"Nonsense," laughed the mayor. "Everybody knows dogs can't paint."